CONTENTS

CHAPTER ONE

THE HIDDEN LIBRARY

Celia had just moved to a new house in a new town. It was the weekend, and she was ready to explore her new neighbourhood.

She followed a dark path through a wooded area. She found a big, old building.

"How odd. It looks like a library," Celia said. "Why would a library be out here?"

LIBRARY ALIVE!

by John Sazaklis

illustrated by Katie Crumpton

Raintree is an imprint of Capstone Global Library Limited, a company
incorporated in England and Wales having its registered office at
264 Banbury Road, Oxford, OX2 7DY – Registered company number:
6695582

www.raintree.co.uk
myorders@raintree.co.uk

Designed by Sarah Bennett
Original illustrations © Capstone Global Library Limited 2022
Originated by Capstone Global Library Ltd
Printed and bound in India

Design Elements: Shutterstock: ALEXEY GRIGOREV, vavectors, Zaie

ISBN 978 1 3982 2323 3

British Library Cataloguing in Publication Data
A full catalogue record for this book is available from the British
Library.

Before Celia could even knock, the door was flung open.

"Welcome!" said a woman with a sneaky smile. "I'm the librarian here, and I love finding the perfect book for every child. Check this one out!"

She pushed the book towards
Celia. The title was *Tricky Tricksters*.
As soon as Celia opened it, there
was a blinding flash of light.
FWOOSH!
Startled, Celia dropped the book.

Light swirled around Celia. The
pages of the book fluttered, and
there was another burst of light.

FWOOSH!

Three men appeared.

"Meet Maui, Loki and Anansi,"
said the librarian. "They are
the trickster gods of myths and
legends."

Celia was scared, but she was also curious.

"And who exactly are *you*?" she asked the woman.

"I am Eris," the woman said. "The Greek goddess of trouble."

"What is going on?" Celia asked.

"I needed a human to help me free my friends from their prison in these pages," answered Eris. "Now that they are here, *your* world is *ours*!"

CHAPTER TWO

LIBRARY MADNESS

"Never!" Celia shouted.

She bravely pushed Eris away.

Anansi changed into a large spider and chased Celia. He called his crew of creepy, crawly creatures to follow him.

Celia ran as fast as she could.

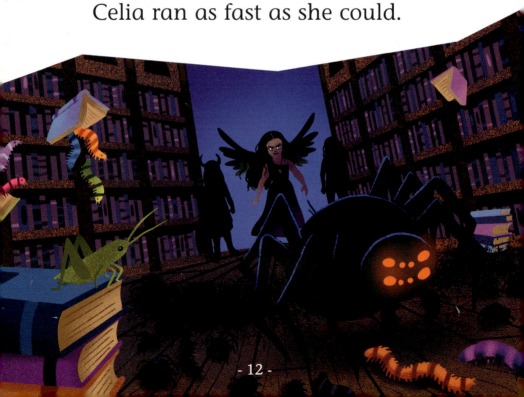

Meanwhile, Maui turned into a hawk. He flew high above Celia and screeched.

SCREEEEEEE!

Celia tripped over a book, and it fell open.

The story about a large beanstalk
came to life. A trunk of twisted vines
shot up. It smashed into Maui!

CRASH!

"This library is alive!" Celia cried.

Vines twisted and turned, covering everything. Anansi and his creepy creatures leapt through the leaves.

"I need to get out of this jungle!" Celia said.

A book about wildlife magically landed in her hand and roared to life! A herd of elephants stampeded over Anansi's creepy army.

CHAPTER THREE

BOOKS TO THE RESCUE

Celia felt brave and bold. She grabbed a pile of books. Suddenly, Loki blocked her path.

"Your little tricks are no match for me," he said.

"Here's a story that will blow you away!" Celia smiled as she opened *The Wonderful Wizard of Oz.*

WHOOSH!

A swirling, whirling tornado lifted up Loki. He landed on the other side of the library.

Suddenly, Eris appeared. The
winged woman was furious!

"Did you think you could defeat
us?" she shouted. "You are just
a human!"

"We are myths! We are legends!"
Maui cried.

"We are the trickiest tricksters!"
Anansi added.

"I have a few tricks of my own,"
Celia said.

Celia opened a book of Greek myths. A snake-haired creature with glowing eyes appeared.

"Meet Medusa," Celia said, her eyes shut tight. "Her stare can turn anyone – or any*thing* – to stone!"

In a blinding flash, Medusa's magic blasted the living library. *FWOOOOSH!*

When Celia opened her eyes, the mysterious building had disappeared.

The sky had cleared. Celia was now surrounded by statues of the terrible tricksters.

"Is this sculpture garden new?" asked a lady walking her dog.

"Yes," Celia answered. "I made it myself."

"You are very talented. How did you make it?" she asked.

"It's quite a story," replied Celia. "Would you like to hear it?"

AUTHOR

John Sazaklis is a *New York Times* bestselling author with almost 100 children's books under his belt! He has also illustrated Spider-Man books, created toys for *MAD* magazine, and written for the BEN 10 animated series. John lives in New York City, USA, with his super-powered wife and daughter.

ILLUSTRATOR

Katie Crumpton ventured to San Francisco, USA, to earn a degree from the Academy of Art University. She enjoys drawing whimsical and magical things and loves to use all the colours of the rainbow to bring her work to life. Magic, nature, animals and outer space are some of the things that inspire her.

GLOSSARY

flutter to move back and forth quickly

legend a story passed down through the years; also, a person who is one of the best at what they do

myth a story from ancient times

sculpture a piece of art made by shaping clay, stone, metal or other material

stampede when a herd of animals suddenly rushes wildly

tornado a storm with powerful winds

whirl to turn around

DISCUSSION QUESTIONS

1. Do you think it was a good idea for Celia to go into the library? What would you have done?

2. If you could pick any book to come to life, what would it be and why?

3. What do you think would have happened if Celia hadn't turned the trickster gods to stone?

WRITING PROMPTS

1. Make a list of your five favourite books.

2. Pretend you are Celia. Write a diary entry about your adventure at the library.

3. The trickster gods each have their own type of superpower. Write about a superpower you would like to have.

SCARED SILLY JOKES!

What building is the tallest?
The library, because it has the most storeys!

What happens when the mummy goes to the library?
He gets wrapped up in a good book.

Why couldn't the boy get into the library?
It was all booked up!

Why did the fish go to the library?
To find some bookworms.

How does a librarian travel?
He books flights.

What is the best job for a book?
An undercover cop

What did the girl think about the Mount Everest book?
She said it was a real cliff-hanger!

Why does the ghost always need more books?
He goes through them too quickly.

BOO BOOKS

Discover more just-right frights!

Only from Raintree